Say Please, Little Bear

This edition published by Parragon Books Ltd in 2015

Parragon Books Ltd
Chartist House
15–17 Trim Street
Bath BA1 1HA, UK
www.parragon.com

ISBN 978-1-4723-7733-3

Printed in China

Say Please, Little Bear

Story by Peter Bently
Illustrations by Robert McPhillips

Parragon

Bath • New York • Cologne • Melbourne • Delhi
Hong Kong • Shenzhen • Singapore • Amsterdam

Daddy Bear and Little Bear were on their
way to playgroup.
But Little Bear kept wandering off.

"Keep hold of my
hand, Little Bear!"
said Daddy Bear.

"Go gently, Little Bear!"
said Daddy Bear at playgroup.

But Little Bear didn't listen.

"Little Bear, it isn't nice to snatch!"

"It's better when
we share, Little Bear,"
said Daddy Bear.

Later, Daddy Bear took Little Bear to
Little Bunny's birthday party.
They went shopping on the way.
"Please hold my hand, Little Bear!"
said Daddy Bear wearily.

Then something in the shop window
gave Daddy Bear an idea.
"Look, Little Bear," he said.
"Mouse wants to speak to us!"

TOY SHOP

"Mouse wants to come to the party too, Little Bear," said Daddy Bear. "But he hates to be late!"

They reached Little Bunny's party on time.
Mouse whispered in Daddy Bear's ear.

"Mouse says, excuse me, please,"
said Daddy Bear.

Little Bear ran to play on the train.
Mouse whispered in Daddy Bear's ear again.
"Mouse says,
can she have
a ride on the
train, please?"

Little Bear snatched the popcorn from his friends.
Mouse whispered in Daddy Bear's ear once again.
"Mouse says, would *you* like some popcorn,
Bunny and Mole?"

When it was
time to go,
Little Bear
stood silently
on the doorstep.
"Mouse says,
thank you for
having me,"
said Daddy Bear.

Little Bear looked at Mouse. Then he looked at Daddy Bear. Then he looked at Little Bunny's mummy and said, "And thank you for having me."

"Oh, thank you for coming, Little Bear,"
smiled Little Bunny's mummy.

"You and Mouse can
come and play any time."

"Mouse likes the way
you said thank you,"
said Daddy Bear.

"And so do I."